FIVE O'CLOCK CHARLIE

Dedicated to Gracie

FIVE O'CLOCK
CHARLIE

By MARGUERITE HENRY
Illustrated by WESLEY DENNIS

) RAND McNALLY & COMPANY · Chicago · New York · San Francisco

CHARLIE was a big old work horse with sad brown eyes and shaggy feathers on his feet. He belonged to Mister Spinks, a lean, weathered man with a fringe of yellow whiskers that almost matched Charlie's mane. They both lived at Tulip Hill Farm in Shropshire, England.

Mister Spinks and everyone else thought Charlie was too old to work. Everyone, that is, except Charlie. He had reached the great age of twenty-eight, but in spite of his years and his dignity, he could still roll over. Not just half way, but a complete once-over! It was tremendous to behold.

And when his rheumatism didn't bother him, he kicked and capered like any frisky colt.

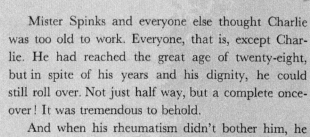

Mister Spinks was a tough yet tender man. He thought a lot of Charlie, who had been a strong puller in his day. So he retired him and gave him a field all to himself, with a nice rain barrel for drinking water. Of course, it was a small field, and nothing

much would grow on it, anyway. Nothing but nasty thistles and chickweed.

Charlie despised them both. One was too prickly, the other too bitter. Quite regularly Mister Spinks managed to bring him a wisp of hay, but even so, Charlie grew hungry and bored with life.

He felt so useless. He missed
the busyness of the old days—
the plowing and planting, the

logging and hauling, the raking and reaping. And he had nowhere at all to go. Not to the millhouse to grind the grain. Nor to the greengrocer's to deliver parsnips and peas and potatoes. Nor to the blacksmith for a new set of shoes. Not even to the old Boar's Head Inn on Cowcross Road.

Perhaps what happened at the Boar's Head was what he missed most of all.

Charlie remembered how every afternoon at the stroke of five Birdie would appear. She was not a bird at all; she was a plump-chested cook in a white apron. She would bounce out of the Inn like a cuckoo from a clock.

Then she would pull a stout rope beside the door, which set a bell to ringing. This meant that the apple tarts were nicely browned and ready to come out of the oven.

Quick as flies the people would come swarming. There were teamsters and tailors, carpenters and cobblers, bankers and barristers, goldsmiths, silversmiths, and blacksmiths.

They came afoot, they came on wagons, they came
in fine carriages. In the courtyard they separated.
Some went indoors, and the others gathered at the
swing-out, swing-in window to the kitchen.

Mister Spinks was one who went inside; he enjoyed a bumper of punch with his apple tart.

Charlie was always left standing at the hitching rail with the lines wrapped loosely around it. He towered above the elegant little hackneys and the workaday cobs.

The moment Mister Spinks disappeared, Charlie used to pull the lines free and lumber over to the swing-in, swing-out window. There he would wait politely

while the two-legged creatures were served. They all slapped him affectionately on the rump as they went back to their carts and carriages.

Then at last it would be Charlie's turn. His nostrils would flutter in excitement as Birdie held out the flat of her hand. On it there was always a beautiful apple tart, oozing with juices that smelled of sugar and spices.

"Charlie, you rascal!" she would exclaim. "Now you get back to the hitching rail and do your eating there. I don't want you slobbering all over my clean window."

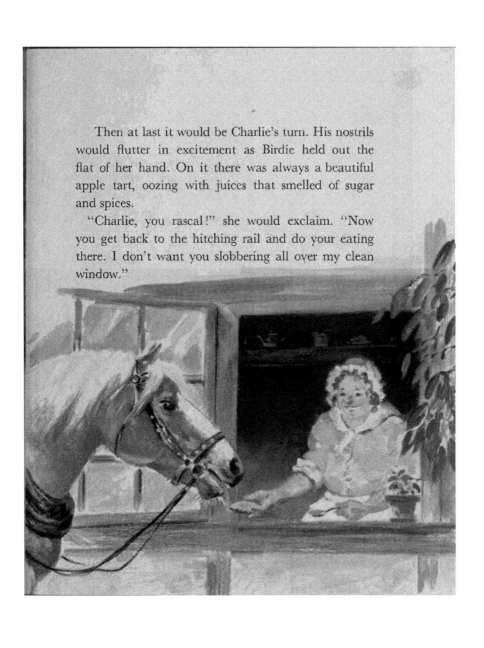

When Mister Spinks finally came out, wiping his whiskers on his sleeve, he never seemed to notice that Charlie's lines were no longer wrapped about the rail. He just hooked him up, climbed onto the seat of the wagon, gave a "cluck-cluck" to Charlie, and off they would go, home to Tulip Hill.

In his retirement Charlie sadly missed this five-o'clock treat. He felt hungry and forlorn in his silent field with only the grasshoppers thrumming their wings together, and a woodpecker drilling holes in an old dead tree.

Morning, noon, and night were all alike. It was a world of nothing but weeds and sky.

Day by day his head drooped lower and his tail hung limp as an old rope.

A month dragged by. Then late one afternoon a curious thing happened. Charlie was aroused from his day-dreaming by the wind. It was blowing sharply, bringing city smells and city sounds. He lifted his head, and suddenly the time-clock in his mind began ringing. It was as if he heard a bell!

He *had* to answer it. He trotted across the field, around the old dead tree, past the water barrel, faster and faster until he broke into a gallop. He was heading straight for the fence, he was going to jump it!

With all his strength and power he collected his great bulk and flung himself up and over, but he was traveling too fast. His forefeet struck the top rail, smashing it to bits.

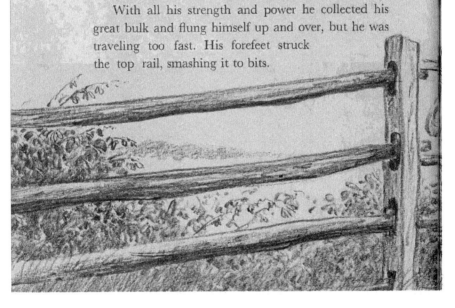

He didn't even feel or hear the crash. He was over! He was free!

In a burst he was down the lane and out upon the pike, galumphing toward the village. His feathers swished. His hoofs clanked. *Kal-lop, kal-lop, kal-lippity klop.*

Stately and bold and full of purpose he trotted gaily around the bend, down through a gap in the hills, past the old steepled church, and into Cowcross Road.

It was just like the old days! There was the friendly Boar's Head Inn and the same jolly people gathering at the window. They seemed delighted to see him and thumped him more affectionately than ever.

"Let's give first place to Charlie," one said.
And they all bowed and made way for him.
When he reached the swing-out, swing-in window,
he bunted it with his nose and came face-to-face with

Birdie. *E-ee-eee-eek!* She almost dropped the plate of apple tarts.

"Charlie!" she cried. "*Char*-lie! *Char*-lie!" And she reached up and kissed him on his nose. Then she chose the biggest, brownest, juiciest tart of all for him.

And she let him eat it right there at the window.

It was better than old times! There was no waiting in line, and no wagon to pull.

Charlie hadn't been so happy in weeks. He trumpeted his joy to the people. Then with a snort of greeting to the unfortunate horses tied at the rail, he galumphed back home at an easy gait, the feathers on his feet swinging in the little breeze he made.

He felt young and frisky again, and his loneliness vanished like a fog when the sun comes out.

Each day now he trotted to the Inn and arrived a jot before five o'clock. And each day he bunted the swing-out, swing-in window and poked his nose into the kitchen. If the kettle was hissing and the dishes

making a clatter, he let out a lusty bugle to make
Birdie notice him. She always jumped and grabbed
herself as if an icicle had dropped down her bosom.

"Lor'-love-a-duck!" she exclaimed. "It must be time to ring the bell. Whatever would I do without you, Charlie?"

And she bounced out of the Inn like the cuckoo from the clock. And soon the bell was binging and bonging, and farmers' wagons were pulling up, and fine carriages were all about, and people were swarming into the Inn for their apple tarts and tea.

Slowly a beautiful thing was happening to Charlie. Birdie began depending more and more on him to remind her when it was tea time. He became her alarm clock.

Then something even more wonderful happened. She taught him how to take the rope between his big yellow teeth and ring the bell himself!

At last he had something important to do! Every day. Rain or shine. Summer or winter.

Of course, Mister Spinks heard about these daily
jaunts. The news traveled to Tulip Hill and well

beyond. And one afternoon as he was sauntering into the Boar's Head, he caught sight of Charlie, large
as life, over at the window. He fancied for a moment
the thought of speaking to Charlie, but he couldn't
quite bring himself to do it. He just gave a wink in
his direction; then, chuckling, he quickly turned his
head, pretending not to see.

It was a kind of secret shared.

In the course of time, Mr. Spinks's wife noticed the broken fence rail. "Land sakes alive!" she exclaimed. "Will you look at what that good-for-nothing Charlie has done! Mind that you mend the fence at once," she scolded Mr. Spinks. In fact, she had to scold him again and again.

Each time he would scratch his head thoughtfully and then reply in the same way. "Quite right, my dear. Some day I'll fix it."

But he never did.

Lightning Source UK Ltd.
Milton Keynes UK
UKHW022229060622
404035UK00010B/221